DATE DUE			

WHO WANTS ONE?

WHO WANTS ONE?

Mary Serfozo
illustrated by Keiko Narahashi

Margaret K. McElderry Books
New York

For John
M.S.

For Mikah and Peter
K.N.

Margaret K. McElderry Books
Macmillan Publishing Company
866 Third Avenue
New York, NY 10022
Collier Macmillan Canada, Inc.

Composition by Linoprint Composition, New York, New York
Printed and bound by Toppan Printing Company in Hong Kong

First Edition
10 9 8 7 6 5 4 3 2 1

Library of Congress Cataloging-in-Publication Data
Serfozo, Mary.
   Who wants one?
   Summary: Rhyming text and illustrations introduce the
numbers one through ten.
   1. Counting—Juvenile literature. [1. Counting]
I. Narahashi, Keiko, ill.   II. Title.
QA113.S47 1989   513'.2 [E]   88-26614
ISBN 0-689-50474-8

Who wants one?

1 Who wants one?
Do you want one?
One butterfly, one raisin bun,
One rainbow coming with the sun.
Do you want one?

YES, I WANT ONE!

2 Well, I like two.
Now won't two do?
Two shiny shoes, two kangaroos,
Two kangaroos in shiny shoes.
Do you want two?

NO, I WANT ONE!

3 Perhaps it's three
you want to see.
Three clocks, three socks, three locks, three keys,
Three treetops tossing in the breeze.
Do you want three?

NO, I WANT ONE!

4 I know…it's four
you're waiting for!
Four goats in boats—just four, no more.
Four bright red boots beside the door.
Do you want four?

NO, I WANT ONE!

5 Or maybe five?
Well, sakes alive!
Five peacocks coming up the drive,
Five black bees buzzing 'round the hive.
Do you want five?

NO, I WANT ONE!

6 Do you pick six?
Look, here is six.
Six sails, six whales, six driftwood sticks,
Six jolly dolphins doing tricks.
Do you want six?

NO, I WANT ONE!

7 Then why not seven,
for heaven's sake?
Seven kites and seven cakes,
And seven swans on sky-blue lakes.
Do you want seven?

NO, I WANT ONE!

8 You might like eight.
I think eight's great.
Eight circus clowns all juggling plates,
Eight teddy bears on roller skates.
Do you want eight?

NO, I WANT ONE!

9 You don't want nine,
when nine's so fine?
Nine bluebirds sitting on a sign,
Nine green umbrellas in a line.
Do you want nine?

NO, I WANT ONE!

10 And now here's ten.
Do you want ten?
Ten speckled eggs from ten brown hens,
Ten pink pigs happy in their pens.
Do you want ten?

NO, I WANT ONE!

Well, now, let's just be sure…
We'll go back
and count again

all the numbers
from one to ten.

1 One

2 Two

3 Three

4 Four

Five 5

Six 6

Seven 7

Eight 8

9 Nine

10 Ten

Tell me again,
now that we're done...

Do you want one?

YES, I WANT ONE!